Start Reading
AND WRITING

The Wonderful Gift

First published in the UK in 2004 by
QED Publishing
A Quarto Group Company
226 City Road
London, EC1V 2TT

www.qed-publishing.co.uk

A Catalogue record for this book is available
from the British Library.

ISBN 1 84538 324 9

Written by Clare Bevan
Designed by Alix Wood
Editor Hannah Ray
Illustrated by Kelly Waldek

Series Consultant Anne Faundez
Creative Director Louise Morley
Editorial Manager Jean Coppendale

Printed and bound in China

Start Reading
AND WRITING

The Wonderful Gift

Clare Bevan

QED Publishing

When the little princess was born, the King and Queen were VERY excited.

"She shall have EVERYTHING she wants," said the King.

"She shall be the happiest princess in the whole world," said the Queen.

They gave her a golden rattle and a teddy bear with soft, silky fur. They rocked her in a silver cradle.

The little princess cried and cried and CRIED.

"Give the little princess a beautiful name," said the Wise Man. "Then she will be happy." So the King and the Queen looked through a big book and chose the most beautiful name they could find.

"She shall be called Princess Starlight," said the Queen.

"Her room shall be decorated with stars," said the King.

Big Book of Names

Princess Starlight cried and cried and CRIED.

One year later, Princess Starlight was STILL crying.
"Give her a birthday party," said the Wise Man.
"Everyone will bring her a present.
Then she will be happy."

So the King wrote letters on shiny paper to all the Fairy Godmothers. The Queen gave Princess Starlight a blue party dress, scattered with stars.

Princess Starlight cried and cried and CRIED.

It was a lovely party. There was a big birthday cake with one candle and hundreds of sugar stars. There were balloons shaped like stars, and a mountain of presents wrapped in starry paper.

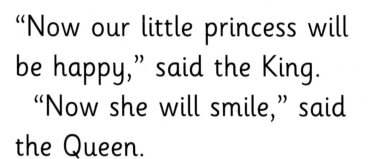

"Now our little princess will be happy," said the King.

"Now she will smile," said the Queen.

Princess Starlight looked at her cake and her balloons and her presents. She was quiet for a whole minute.

Then she started to cry.

11

The Fairy Godmothers said, "We will give our presents
to Princess Starlight. Then she will be happy."
They gave her a tiny flying horse, a talking mirror
that could tell jokes, a crown made of moonbeams
and a box of magic jewels.

Princess Starlight looked at
her presents for a long time.
Everyone held their breath.
Then she CRIED.

Many years went by.

Princess Starlight still wore beautiful dresses scattered with stars. Inside her starry room, she kept her magical presents.

Every day, jesters and jugglers tried to make her smile.

Every day, the King and Queen tried to make her happy.

But STILL she felt sad and wanted to cry.

One day, she heard
someone singing
outside her window.
"Who is THAT?"
she asked grumpily.

Princess Starlight stamped down the palace stairs to see the King and Queen. "Someone is making an AWFUL noise outside my window," she grumbled. "You must stop him at once."

"Of course," said the King and Queen. "If it will make you happy."

So the palace policeman found the singer and marched him indoors. It was the gardener's son. He looked very grubby, but he had twinkly eyes.

"Why are you so happy?"
asked Princess Starlight crossly.

The gardener's son smiled. "Because the sun is shining and the flowers are growing," he answered.

"I don't understand," said Princess Starlight with a frown. "I have all my treasures, yet I feel sad."

"That is because you do not have the Wonderful Gift of Happiness," said the gardener's son.

"Where can we find this Wonderful Gift?" asked the King and Queen.

"Princess Starlight must find it for herself," said the gardener's son.

He led Princess Starlight outside and showed her how to dig the earth. Together, they planted seeds and sang funny songs. They worked for many weeks.

One day, Princess Starlight ran indoors. She was grubby, but she was smiling and her arms were full of starry flowers.

"I still haven't found the Gift of Happiness," she laughed.

But, of course, she had. Hadn't she?

What do you think?

What do the King and Queen look like? Can you describe them?

The Fairy Godmothers gave Princess Starlight some magical presents. Can you remember what they were?

What words would you use to describe the gardener's son?

Did Princess Starlight find the Gift of Happiness? How?

Carers' and teachers' notes

- Read the story together. Why was Princess Starlight so cross and grumpy?
- Talk about presents. Do expensive toys make children happy?
- Make a list of things that do make people happy, for example, spending time with friends, or playing games.
- Find words in the text that show how Princess Starlight was feeling, for example, 'grumpy', 'sad'.
- Find words that describe how people speak, for example, 'asked', 'grumbled'.
- Encourage your child to imagine some magical presents that a fairy godmother could give.
- Together, invent a story about someone who is sad. Think of all sorts of funny ways to make the sad person smile or laugh.
- Turn your funny story into a comic strip with speech bubbles. Encourage your child to draw and colour the pictures for the comic strip. Help your child to write the dialogue for the speech bubbles.
- Invent a 'Happiness' spell. What would it contain? For example, a hug, a kind word, a ride on a roundabout, an ice-cream, a funny joke.
- In this story, making friends with the gardener's son, playing in the garden and growing flowers made Princess Starlight happy. Encourage your child to describe an activity that makes him/her happy. For example, painting a picture or helping you to bake a cake.
- Together, write a 'Happy Poem'. Take it in turns to suggest a happy line. But don't worry if it doesn't rhyme!
- Together, find a tune to turn your 'Happy Poem' into a song.